DARK WATER: BEAMING SMILE

DARK WATER: BEAMING SMILE

KEVIN JAMES BREAUX

Write Makes Might!

The water smelled horrible, like moldy rotting wood. I covered my nose with a handkerchief that I found in my husband's rain jacket just to filter the air. You see, I really wished that was the only stench around, but it wasn't. Occasionally, my nose caught a hint of something else, something long deceased. I figured it might be a skunk or raccoon; something that had died weeks before the rains hit us, but then washed up during the floods. There were farms all around my home, so that stink must've belonged to a dead animal. I tried to convince myself that it could've been livestock; a goat or cow even, but truth be told, I wasn't sure. Even had I wanted to, I couldn't see past the edges of my house; it was just too dammed dark.

The sky had finally stopped dumping rain about an hour ago. It was midnight or possibly a little later, as far as I could guess with no watch on my wrist. Funny that I would look at my wrist; I hadn't owned a watch in maybe ten years. The only jewelry I had was my wedding ring, and that had left my finger hours ago.

Seventy-two hours of relentless downpouring and here I was alone in the dark, atop the pitch of my roof with nothing but a dying flashlight and my thoughts.

I should've left Montgomery County when I had the chance, I swore inside my head for the hundredth time since I climbed up here. I should've blazed out of this shithole town the first moment I could... but I didn't. "You's a lazy girl, Sarah," my father used to sing when I was just a small child. I guess he was right, because I had my chance to leave after school was finished, and I didn't take it.

Back then, my best friend Hilly was departing for college and offered me a ride out of town at the end of that week. I told her I'd catch up with her in a day or two, let her know my decision, but that one day, became another, and another. Before I knew it years were gone, and I carried a child inside my belly.

I never intended this to happen; in fact, I despised it. But damn-it-all I had become my mother.

A loud thump rattled me from my thoughts. I spun around and clicked on my flashlight, but the weak bulb barely lit more than two feet in front of me. Worthless, and still I didn't toss it into the murky flood waters below, where all the other trash from the neighborhood was. Something about that flashlight's presence in my hand; the long metal shaft, the bulbous end, it made me feel safe. It was my weapon, a mighty hammer to swing if I needed to protect myself.

Another thump startled me. I pinpointed it this time; it's against the back side of my house. That noise, it must've been a large piece of debris, maybe a chunk of wood from our old barn. The barn, for heaven's sake, felt like its collapse was days ago. That was a sight I wouldn't soon forget. That old barn had been in my family's possession for many, many years.

∗∗∗

It was soon after a large swell of water broke against my house. I was upstairs getting my boys ready to evacuate town while Joseph, my husband, was supposed to be getting the old Bronco fired up. I heard Joseph scream through the whipping winds that the truck was stalled. When I opened the window to yell back at him, my ears filled with the sound of the barn rumbling. I watched in awe as the flood water rushed hard against the barn's foundation. The building moaned like an old man standing as it suddenly lurched upward, and then promptly folded down upon itself, no sturdier than a house of cards.

Our truck was in there, was all I could think; the Bronco, our only means of transportation. I'm totally trapped here now. There was no escape. Joseph waved his arms wildly breaking my stare upon the rubble broken. He pointed off to the side of the house and drew my attention off to our trailer. Joseph might not have looked it, often mistaken for just another "good ole boy," but he was a forward thinker. He'd pushed our trailer out of the barn moments before it collapsed. He saved his little fishing boat, a rusty hunk of trash he called the Missouri Minnow.

***

There was that noise again. It sounded soft, not like a wooden beam or other piece of hard debris as I first imagined it was. I crept across the roof carefully; my shoes were soaked and their grip on the slick shingles was iffy at best. If I was to survive until a rescue team arrived, I'd need to stay out of that dark water.

THUMP. THUMP.

I heard it again as I inched my way to the back of my house. I could see the water levels had reached up to the windows on the second story of the house. There was no doubt in my mind that the flood water had filled the inside all the way to the attic by now. Everything inside was ruined. All those memories gone; I'd certainly have no reason to—*THUMP.*

God, that sound was loud.

After I shook the flashlight a few times, I pointed it down toward the back door off the kitchen. The darkness of the night and the pitch-black water swallowed almost every inch of illumination the flashlight gave me. A pack of matches or an old cigarette lighter would've worked as good, I supposed.

I gazed down for some time at the edge of my house. The flood water churned around; it moved like the gentle waves of that bay in the Gulf of Mexico my parents once took me to when I was ten.

There in the water was a kerosene tank, probably the one we had in the barn. It bobbed up and down like a buoy, occasionally clanging against the house, but it wasn't making that weird thud. As my eyes examined the tank, I heard my mystery sound. It was so close I felt it rattle my ears. I pivoted my body to the right, faced where the sound came from, and inched myself to the tip of the roof above the back door. When I peered down, my fading flashlight revealed something large and furry.

What was it? I'd seen bear before, but this seemed bigger, exceeding the size of my tiny spotlight. I panned the dark brown fur from end to end. It was a tall bear, but not as beefy as most. It must have been sick. Maybe the thing had starved to death before the flood, I thought. As I stared, my flashlight's bulb surged up revealing two long spindly limbs, almost like human arms.

I jumped back and fell hard to my butt. The impact jarred the only source of light I had from my hand and sent it rolling loudly over the side of the roof. When the flashlight hit the water, hell I half expected to hear someone yell out my name when they heard that loudness. With my breath held down into my stomach, I waited for the full count of ten Mississippi for a voice to call to me from the darkness, yet none came. Unlike me, my neighbors left when the getting was good.

My lungs drew in the sour air and pushed it out as fast as they could. Good thing I quit smoking when the boys were born, or I wouldn't only be cold, and wet, but wheezing in pain up here too. Carefully, I retreated to my original spot on the roof and still I couldn't help but face the back where I saw the dead animal.

An image of its wet, hair-covered body was born in my mind each time I heard the thumping sound. I couldn't empty my head of the sight, and soon I began to question myself. *THUMP.*

Maybe I was wrong, maybe this wasn't a bear after all. Its fur seemed too long, so much so it clumped into spiky ends. I assumed it was a bear from its size, but the more I thought about the shape, it was all wrong. *THUMP.*

It was so damn skinny. God—what was it?

The rain came back, further soaking me. I praised God it was July, for the nights stayed somewhat warm. I remembered a time when I was fourteen and camped out all night with a friend. It was early October, and the pair of us nearly caught our deaths after getting drenched by a passing storm. I had a cough and the sniffles for a month. The thought made me laugh. My mother said to the day she died, "No medicine found in the drug store can cure stupidity."

THUMP.

I drew my knees into my body and wrapped my rain jacket around all my limbs in efforts to keep warm. Help should be coming soon, I thought. Slowly, I braced myself against the chimney. I tried to close my eyes and sleep.

THUMP. THUMP. THUMP.

Every time I felt myself drifting off, the banging sound rang out in my ear. It almost sounded like it was getting closer. I tried to shut it out of my head, but my mind kept returning to it. What was it? A sickly cow? Perhaps it was a big wolf? I just had to know what that decaying thing was I saw. I needed to know if it was what I smelled.

THUMP.

I should've left town when I had the chance. I should've gone with Hilly. I should've run for it, left it all behind me, never looked back. God, all that was twelve years ago, I'm thirty now. I couldn't just up and leave, could I? I loved my children with all my heart and soul; how could I do that to them? Yet still, when I looked at my boys, Jimmy and Jonny, I often wondered if my mother settled for me, like I settled for them.

The noise rattled me again; it was nearing dawn. Had I slept? I couldn't tell. Would help be here soon?

"I should've left town when I had the chance!"

I shouted as I watched the sunrise. Suddenly, the shadows were lifted, and the veil of darkness was gone. I could see everything around me. All the destruction, the litter...the sewage. Turns out, I soon preferred the darkness. Now that I could see everything, my situation was even more real. I was going to die up here, wasn't I?

Out near the street, I spotted a body bobbing up and down; caught, no doubt, on our old white picket fence. That fence needed to be torn out years ago and replaced with a new one, but Joseph wanted to just repaint it. I told him don't bother, just tear it down. I would prefer no fence, to that same old one just repainted. While watching the stuck body, bobbing up and down, I realized just how glad I was he didn't listen to me. The water still flowed in my direction and that person, I think it was old man Rutherford, would've been banging up against my house along with the dead—hold up a moment, I hadn't heard the thumping for a bit.

I stood up quickly, asking my legs to hold the weight of my body, yet they weren't ready, and I fell forward to my knees, nearly sliding off the roof. I screamed as I clapped my hand to the wet shingles and held myself still. I wasn't going to fall in that disgusting water; I would sooner kill myself before that happened.

Too scared to stand again, I crawled across my rooftop to the back of the house so I could finally look at the bear that had been floating dead in the water. Or was it a wolf? My mind prepared me for the sight. I imagined all sorts of horrors, things I had seen in scary movies when I was a child. Whatever grotesqueness was about to welcome my eyes wouldn't overwhelm me; I could handle it. I'd seen worse.

When I peeked over the edge of the roof, I saw nothing. Just some trash, a few chunks of wood from the barn, something that looked like an old, rusty toaster, and a cardboard box with the label "Seed" on it. The animal was gone. As I stood, my eyes brushed over something entirely unexpected. The water had receded some and the top of the lower roof was exposed. To my surprise, atop that tiny peak, curled up into a near fetal position, was a young naked girl.

I should've been shocked at the girl's presence below me, but instead of recoiling in fright, I was compelled to stare. I couldn't see her face; it was covered in her long curly wet hair. Was she alive or dead?

"Hey you," I called down to her, but she didn't respond so I yelled louder. "Hey! Hey!"

I figured she must be dead. She must've been tossed around so much in the flood that the water tore her clothing from her body. It happens; I had read about it once, year's back, on the scandal sheets when a pair of celebrity girls got caught up in some rapids while rafting. That poor girl, I thought as I stared at her, she probably drowned. She suffocated; gasped for air when there was none... What a horrible way to go.

The morning sun was warm, so I removed my husband's rain jacket. Atop the roof, I chose not to stare in the direction of the destruction and filth and instead just look at the girl. She seemed so peaceful down there, like a sleeping baby. I wished I could sleep so soundly, but the air smelled so bad I could almost taste it. My stomach rumbled; what a time to be hungry. With my nerves as they were...yuck, the thought of eating made me nauseous. When would I be rescued?

The sun crept up into the heights of the sky while I sat and gazed at the girl. I wondered who she was, what her age was, was she in love? What was her life like? Was she happy, truly happy? Did she know what true happiness was? I didn't when I was her age. I must've cried three times. That poor, young girl. We had a lot in common; she never escaped this town either.

I looked away for a moment to dry my red eyes. I considered one of two options; I had to do something for her. I could not bury her, so I had to lay her body to rest in another fashion. I could push her off that little ledge into the water. Maybe she'd sink or be pulled away when the water receded again. She deserved better. Maybe some flowers and a nice obituary, but I had neither to give.

My second idea was a little more personal. Part of me wanted to put her body in my house, where it'd be protected. There was a small window above the toilet in my master bathroom and it sat open a crack not two feet above the ledge she was on. All I would have to do is squeeze her in through that narrow window and then close it up behind her. My house was ruined anyway so why not, right? At least she would be safe there until she got a proper burial.

I looked all around, skimming the horizon with my eyes. There was no sign of my husband, the police, or the National Guard. I had to do something. It was beginning to feel like I'd be here on my roof for a while longer, maybe even the rest of the day. Geez, I had not even seen a helicopter fly anywhere nearby. I didn't want to be still any longer; I didn't want to feel so powerless in my misfortune, so I carefully climbed down to the peak the young woman was on.

"Girlie, you have my deepest sympathy. Whole world ahead; this shithole town's no place for a final resting."

After I knelt beside her, I brushed the wet, dirty blonde hair from her face. Holy shit, I knew her. Jasmine: Her name was Jasmine. Oh, what was her last name again? I could almost hear it in my head, like a distant echo. Her mother and father had split up a few years back. She was sixteen at the time. Before that, she had babysat for me three times, sweet girl, very quiet. Whinstone, that's it; Jasmine Whinstone.

Now that I knew who she was I found myself staring again. Last time I saw her she was a beanpole of a girl, tall and skinny. It was clearly apparent she had filled out in the past three years. Her body, so young and new, reminded me of the girls in the Fredericks of Hollywood catalogues my husband got twice a year. You know, skinny, yet with enough curves to make a bikini pop.

Sure, Jasmine was a little plain for looks, but her physique would've fit that Fredericks lingerie perfectly. Maybe it's a good thing my husband wasn't here, or he would have gotten an eye full. Was that jealousy I felt, maybe it was, hmmm-that's kinda funny.

While I brushed the hair from her face again, I noticed a hint of warmth in her cheek. I paid it no mind, still caught up in my own thoughts. Slowly, I traced her upper and lower lips with my index finger. Wait, what was that? I swore I felt a tiny quiver. She moved. The shock of her lazily swatting my hand from her face jolted my legs with enough energy to instantly stand me up.

"Sweet Jesus, you're alive!" I screamed, not meaning to.

Jasmine's eyes fluttered under her eyelids a moment before they slowly peeled open. She didn't look at me at first. Before she cast her gaze my way, she looked at her hands. She turned them over and over as she examined them, if only for a moment, before she planted them both firmly on the shingles above where her head had just rested. Jasmine slid her knees under herself as she arched her back in a stretch like a dog waking from a nap.

"Why me?" she yawned while she bowed her back upward.

I wanted to speak, but I found no words. I just watched as she stood up and braced herself against the side of my house. I wondered if she even knew I was there, since she seemed entranced by her reflection in my bathroom window.

"What happened?"

Was she talking to me? I hesitated to speak and when I didn't answer her, she twisted her head to me, and her wet hair flopped over her eyes again when the wind caught it.

"What happened to me?" she repeated, her voice so low I almost couldn't hear it.

"What? I-I you were—" I stuttered.

"Oh God where am I? How did I get here?" She shook as she spit out question after question.

I guess you could say my maternal instincts kicked in, because I felt a deep concern for her as if she was one of my children.

"Easy girl, watch your step we're on a roof."

"A roof?"

I saw her eyes widen through the panic; she hadn't realized it until now. Now, grasping at the window frame, she searched for something solid to hold on to.

"You're safe now. Here, take my hand."

I reached out to her and when I did, I could see something click in her head. I think it was at that very moment that she remembered me. I don't blame her. I was a mess; a shade of the person I was a day ago, let alone three years. Back then, the last time we held each other's company, I had longer hair and was all prettied up for the State Fair. Come to think of it, that was the last night Joseph, and I went out, three years and some months ago.

"You? Mrs. Ros—"

"Sarah." I interrupted her.

Jasmine took my hand in hers. The sensation of her warm skin struck me as odd. I guess I expected her to be a touch colder, having spent the night down there in the murky waters...nude.

"Lord, how did I get here?" she said as she patted her open hands down her stomach to her hips where her pant pockets would have been. "Did you see—"

"There was a flash flood. I reckon you were caught up in it; must have swept your clothes clear off."

Jasmine gazed down at herself, then back up at me. Had our roles been reversed, I think I would've made efforts to cover myself, chest to crotch, but she did not. Maybe I was a little insecure, maybe it was this younger generation. I had this thought before, last time I was at the market, that girls these days seemed more confident with their bodies. Jasmine, she seemed at home naked. Gosh, how she'd grown, last time I saw her she was so reserved and proper. I couldn't help but wonder what had changed.

"I have a rain jacket up on the pitch, you could wear it."

I know she heard me, because she nodded, but her attention was gone. Eyes cast out far into the submerged fields behind where my old barn used to sit. She just kept nodding as I talked.

"Let's climb back up there together. I'll help you up."

"S-okay Mrs. Sarah, I'm a good climber, runs in the family."

Family. As I recall, hers had a nasty split. Her parents' divorce was the talk of the town. I remember it well. One day her mother had made a big stink in the grocery store. She screamed and threw glass bottles of strawberry jelly all around, going on like a true lunatic. No one was sure what was wrong with her, but the checkout girl told me later that she thought the woman had gone mad or at least was stone drunk. Later that week, the police were at their home. Reports of domestic abuse and a pair of photos hit our newspapers the following morning. Both Jasmine's Ma and Pa had bruises and cuts on their faces and arms. It was a sad thing to see.

"I used to climb the apple tree outside my home all the time. My dad says the first time he saw me climb it I was four. He tells me it was the darnedest thing he'd ever seen. You scooted up the side of that tree like a baby bear and reached the perfect crook to rest in, that's what he would tell me over and over."

I watched her pull herself up to the rooftop beside me with little effort. By the time I put my hand out to help her, she had both feet firmly planted on the peak and was wiping her dirty hands on her hips. Her father was plainly right.

"My husband's rain jacket is a little big on me, so it should cover you up all nice and fine."

Jasmine stepped her feet around in a small circle so she could see every direction. She made a sour face as she stared off into the mess of muddy water and bobbing debris. She could smell it too, I'm sure. God, it all just stunk to high heaven, but at least there was a tiny breeze to move the air about.

She didn't rush to put the jacket on as I imagined I would in her circumstance. She held it to her side while she gazed down my street. I felt a little weak, so I sat myself on the wet roof and closed my eyes a moment to empty my head.

"I was clear on the other side of Interstate 94. What the hell brought me all the way out here?"

"Your dad lives out that way, right?"

"We both do. Mother took the house, so we moved into a mobile home in Starkenberg few years back."

"Jasmine, I never got to tell you I was sorry. Last time you sat for my kids was a month or so before—"

"No, it's okay, not like it was your fault."

"I know, I'm just sorry you had to deal with all that at such an age. A girl needs to be a girl, live her own life..."

I gave myself away, my tone of voice, the way my words shook halfway through. I hoped she was too young to be so empathic, but she noticed it, I could see it in the way she looked at me.

"Mighty comfortable without yah clothes," I tried to take the focus off me and put it back on her. "Do you mind? Kinda hard having a conversation while you're bare as a newborn baby."

"Sorry, not often I get this opportunity."

I put forth my best efforts not to stare at her, but as the minutes flew by, and she stayed buck naked, I gave up.

"You ever wish you could just escape the confines of your reality,

Mrs. Sarah? Do whatever you want, whenever you want?" Jasmine said, still facing the road.

"Every day."

"Sometimes, I hate feeling confined within my own skin. I guess you could say I'm one of those people who cannot deal with being crowded."

"Claustrophobic?" I knew exactly how she felt.

"That's it."

She took her eyes off the distance and finally looked down at me. We held the most uncomfortable eye contact I'd ever had with another person. It was even more itchy-twitchy than when Joseph and I had the talk about not having any more children two years ago. Worse than that, oh my, I never would've imagined it possible.

When she finally raised the jacket to her shoulders, she slipped one and then the other arm into the sleeves. The jacket, as I guessed it would, reached her down to mid-thigh and would have kept her private bits covered had she cinched it shut at the waist.

"I'll let you in on a little secret. The flood did not take my clothes."

Her statement made me feel a little odd; I held quiet for a time, and she did too. I couldn't help but sense a kinship for her, one I had not felt for another person in years and I started to realize why. Jasmine reminded me of myself when I was young: curious, rebellious, stupid, and lost.

"You don't have to explain yourself to me, Jasmine. I'm not here to judge you sweetie."

"Then you'd be the first person."

My curiosity about her had overcome my feelings of hunger. For the moment, I had forgotten where I was and thought only about who she was. I figured the best way to find out more about her was to offer more of myself.

"I was just twenty when I got pregnant. I wanted to be free, but I became, as you said, confined by my own skin. Do you have a boyfriend, Jasmine?"

"Me? Oh-no, how could I? I mean I—"

"Your father's real strict, isn't he?" I guessed.

"You think I meant that a boy took my clothes? You think that I was foolin' around when the flood hit?" she smirked and pointed at me playfully.

The thought had crossed my mind, I mean at her age, it was what I was doing.

"Where's your husband then, Mrs. Sarah?"

"When the flood hit, he had his little fishing boat out. He took the boys and motored away. He went down the street, you know, toward town."

"Why didn't you go with him?"

"It's a very small boat. I told him it would be safer if they went on without me."

"You didn't want the boat to tip over."

"That's right." I lied. Why did I lie? "I wanted them to go on without me."

When my mouth had finally spit out the words, Jasmine responded simply by sitting down next to me. She didn't say anything, and she didn't have to. I could read it on her young face; there was an eagerness to hear more of what I had to say. Living with Joseph I had grown used to not having a good listener in my life.

"Truth be told, I was hoping, before the flood got so bad that I had to climb up here, to actually—"

I couldn't believe I was actually saying it out loud.

"Run away?"

Jasmine guessed it.

I had seen the flood as a perfect opportunity to escape my miserable life, but I did it again—I took too long. Why didn't I leave when I had the chance?

***

As I was preparing to leave, to finally escape, a wave of rushing water struck my house hard. I was knocked clear off my feet and tumbled down the stairs into the water that had broken through the first-floor windows and door.

Cold, thick water... almost syrupy. I screamed, at the moment grossed out by that disgusting water on my face, but before my holler ended, I wailed; cried with the pain of disappointment. I knew then I missed my chance.

****

"My life shouldn't be like this."

"How should it be, Mrs. Sarah?"

"I guess more like yours, Jasmine. Boundless," I told her. "Free to do whatever I want, whenever I want. Free to run naked in the rain like you were."

"You know once freedom is lost, you got to fight to get it back. I'm sorry, Mrs. Sarah, but you don't look like much of a fighter to me."

Such comments like that, I started to wonder...who where you Jasmine, a Godsend or the Devil come to test me?

"He-Joseph, he was abusive. I..."

Jasmine reached for my hand to comfort me; I found it funny how our roles had unexpectedly reversed.

"He hurt you?"

"Describe hurt."

Jasmine stood abruptly. I wasn't sure if she'd seen something or if she was just so fueled with what I told her she had to move. Either way, I soon followed. I stood and turned at the waist to look about. I saw nothing.

"What was it?"

"I thought I heard something is all, sorry to interrupt."

"No, I'm done. Done worrying about it, done talking about it. It's grown past time I did something."

Jasmine smiled for the first time since she woke up on the roof over my back door. Her smile lit up the sky and seemed to give the grey clouds a run for their money. Since it had been so long since I'd seen her, I couldn't remember her smile. She was so shy back then; maybe I'd never been graced with such warmth and happiness from her before. I just didn't know, come to think of it, thinking in general was getting kinda hard. I must've been more tired than I thought.

"You have the prettiest smile, Jasmine."

"Thank you. My mother once said if it weren't for my smile, the boys wouldn't look at my face."

"That's not a very nice thing for a mother to say."

"Nah—I always took it as her way of complimenting my boobs."

"Still, that's mean of her."

It started to drizzle again and quickly built back up to a full-fledged rain. Without my raincoat—my hair, the only thing dry on me, would get soaked. I thought of asking for it back. Especially since Jasmine stood there with her head tilted back, the rain cascading down her face and pouring over her chest through the untied jacket. She was barely using it at all and getting the inside all wet no doubt.

"Jasmine..."

"You really should try this," she said as she took the jacket off and tossed it to the side. "It's not that cold out, it's rather warm."

"What are you doing?"

"Freedom, right? That's what you want... isn't it? You said so. There's nothing more liberating than running fully uninhibited in the pouring rain."

"You're gonna catch a cold all soaking wet out here," I laid down excuse number one, and then number two. "Anyway, what if a helicopter flies over, someone comes to rescue us?"

"Worse things could happen," she said. "Right?"

Jasmine was right. Worse things could and have happened. This whole flood had been a blessing and a curse.

"What the hell."

The rain had already soaked my hair and had begun to drip down my back. I had nothing to lose, not like I was gonna get any wetter without my clothes. As I disrobed, I hung my clothing off the old TV antenna. When I got down to my underwear, I paused. Jasmine had been smiling the entire time I undressed, but once again her attention was drawn out past the street. I started to panic; was someone coming? When I reached for my shirt, she spoke out.

"Stop being silly, Mrs. Sarah, ain't no one out there."

"You sure?"

"Counting the corpse across the road, I see only three of us."

"Ha-ha."

There was that smile again. If Jasmine put on some makeup and did her hair, I bet she could've given the beauty queens a run for their money. I waited for her to look away before I removed my bra, yet still, even after it was off, I kept my breasts covered.

"Good, now give yourself to the rain. Shut out everything else and give yourself to it," Jasmine said as she stepped behind me and pivoted me toward the rain by my shoulders.

I closed my eyes and turned my face right into the rain drops, just as I had seen her do. At first, it felt no different than a shower head blasting me with water. Yet, the longer I held still, and pushed out all the other sounds and sensations, I started to notice the subtle differences. The rainwater was warmer and did not strike my face as much as caress it. Unlike the shower, which focused on the spray of water, I felt the steady massage of rain drops all over my body.

When I opened my eyes, Jasmine had my shirt held up to her face in a crumbled-up ball. With a huffing motion she sniffed it, practically inhaling it with deep breaths.

"What the hell are you doing?"

"Just confirming my suspicions."

What the fuck did she mean by that? Confused and uncomfortable I snatched my bra and pants off the rooftop and started to get dressed again.

THUMP.

The sound, oh my God, it was back.

"Did you hear that?" I asked Jasmine as I buttoned up my blue jeans.

"A thumping sound, yeah I heard it."

"Last night, I heard that sound over and over. When I checked it out, I found some strange bear or cow or something."

THUMP. THUMP.

I took my shirt from her hands as I walked by her to the rear of my house.

"It's coming from back here."

I peeked hesitantly over the corner expecting to see that hairy animal I spotted last night, but when my frantic eyes found nothing, I turned back to Jasmine hoping she might have had better luck. Still back near the chimney, I watched her wipe her face on the sleeve of my husband's rain jacket.

"I don't think the sound is coming from over there."

Jasmine knelt near the rim of the roof. She grasped the gutter in both hands, and she leaned forward over the edge. I watched as she snaked her body further over, until she was almost bent over past her waist.

"This window here, it's your bedroom, right?"

"Yeah. Why?"

Jasmine sighed loudly, "Well I found your thumping sound."

"Wh-what is it?"

After she pulled herself back up, she answered me. "I really think you should see for yourself."

I did as she did. I leaned over the edge of the roof. My mind was a clutter of thoughts and images. This storm had really worn me out. My arms ached as I hung there looking in and around the window to my bedroom. Water sloshed about occasionally escaping through a broken windowpane. As I suspected, the flood water inside my house was almost all the way to the ceiling and everything I owned and once cared for, floated about at the top. As I gazed in, I heard the thump and with the sound my eyes discovered the source.

Up and down bobbed Joseph's body. His head bounced off the ceiling underneath me like a dribbling basketball. How did he get into the bedroom? I asked myself over and over. How did he get into the bedroom, when I killed him in the kitchen? Was this what Jasmine wanted me to see? Should I scream? Or pretend I had no clue why a corpse was locked up in my house? Or should I just tell her the truth?

I pulled myself back up onto the rooftop and held my breath for a moment while I thought of what to say.

"He's dead," Jasmine announced. "Your husband's dead."

"I know."

"You killed him—didn't you?"

"I-I don't..."

"That's why I'm fucking here," she spit out her words while pointing at me. "Fucking shit!"

"What?"

Jasmine's actions confused me again. She knew I killed my husband, and from the sounds of it she knew from the get-go. I guess there was no reason for lies anymore.

I told her how this flood was my last chance; a perfect opportunity delivered to me by Mother Nature herself. I explained to her how I suddenly realized that I could kill him and there'd be no evidence; everything would be washed clean by the flood. I talked and talked, and she just stood there listening to me, as intently as ever, so my mouth just kept going.

I even told her exactly how it happened...

* * *

I was carrying a bunch of things out the door when Joseph started yelling at me to pack some food for him to eat while on his pathetic little boat. I told him there was no time, but he wouldn't listen, he just screamed in my face. He told me to shut up and listen.

Terrified that he might hit me if I said another word, I put down the box in my hands and when I did the flashlight tumbled out. I picked the thing up by its cold shaft, my fingers, which wrapped around it, did not even cover a quarter of its length, yet it still felt sturdy inside my hand. While raising the flashlight back up to the box, Joseph walked in front of me. I reacted without thought and swung the thing like a mace into the back of my husband's skull. *THUMP!*

The metal crushed his head like an egg and sent him falling face-first to the ground. His whole body shuddered and bounced atop the floor like a fish out of water. Then it went still. It went silent. He was dead—that bastard was really dead.

***

"You murdered your husband." Jasmine coldly stated the facts.

"I-I did."

"What did you do to your children, Mrs. Sarah?"

Oh my God, what've I done? As she asked me the question, my house shifted. The water had finally broken its foundation. Tossed to the side, the two of us fought a moment to regain our balance.

"I'm sorry Mrs. Sarah, truly I am, but this is why I'm here."

"You said that before. I don't understand."

Jasmine covered her eyes with her hand, while she paced a few steps back and forth. She rubbed the bridge of her nose and spoke slowly. "I don't always understand either."

My admission had clearly bothered her. She walked around in tiny circles, looked down and then back up to the sky. Where had the day gone? I finally noticed it was already dusk and the sun would fully set soon. Where was everyone? Where was my fucking rescue?

"You're a murderer."

"I-I survived years of abuse. There was no—"

"Mrs. Sarah, you need to know something," she interrupted me. "I'm not the girl you knew."

"What are you saying, Jasmine?"

"I'm saying that I was called to you last night, but apparently the flood kept me from reaching you."

"You were called to me?"

"Yes... no," she shook her head. "Not me, the thing I am. God, why, why must this fucking continue to happen to me? Why can't it just stop? When will it stop?"

She babbled again, just like she did when she first woke up. There was something off with her, maybe it was drugs, or maybe it was just the effects of the stress of her parents' divorce. Either way, I was starting to feel like I could no longer share my rooftop with her.

"Jasmine, sweetie, look, there's something else. The boat. My husband's boat, its motor may or may not work, but a strong girl like you could easily paddle it to town. You could get out of here, find us help."

"Wait, I thought…"

"If you look carefully out past those trees across the street, it's wedged between two pines. You see it, that glimmer out there, that's it. You could easily swim out there and push it through."

"Where are your children, Mrs. Sarah?"

"Gone."

"What?"

"I sent them away!" I screamed. "They are dead, okay!"

"What happened to them?"

I started to cry, but I wasn't sure exactly why. I knew all along the raging waters would claim them. Still, I had been numb since I saw the boat capsize. I'd felt nothing. Not even the freedom I expected.

"The flood waters claimed them, okay? I put them on the boat and watched them cross the road. I don't know, I guess the current took them off. After the impact with those trees the thing tipped over, they both fell into the water and vanished. I tried to spot them, but I couldn't, the water was just too damn dark."

"Mrs. Sarah—"

"Oh God, my boys are gone," I said and then finally admitted it. "I didn't put life vests on them. They drowned… Dead."

Jasmine just stared blankly at me. It was as if her eyes had clouded over; she looked empty, soulless. I seemed to have upset her so badly that her body shut down or did it.

"What's wrong with you?" I asked because Jasmine visibly trembled.

"I can't control it."

Jasmine groaned as she began speaking and when her words ended a howling sound escaped her mouth. She sounded like she was in agony. It was a sound I recalled making once myself, the night I was in labor, the night my first child was born. That deep groan: it frightened me then as much as it does now.

Jasmine moaned louder as she doubled over and heaved like someone with the flu.

"God, no!" she screamed.

From my short distance from the girl, I could see red lines, like track marks, form on her arms and legs. Darker and longer by the second, the lines, which I thought might have been protruding veins, weren't that at all, they were something more resembling...seams.

"What are you?" I shouted at her as the lines I saw on her limbs slowly split open.

"I'm her adjudicator and her assassin," Jasmine mumbled through labored breaths.

On her hands and knees, I witnessed her skin crack and peel away; under it was something else, oh God, it was fur. As the clunks of flesh fell off her thin body, a new shape took form. Her skin, it wasn't really her, it was just a covering... a mask. She—it shook like a wet dog. The beast that wore her flesh like a cloak only a moment ago cleared itself of the gore that covered it before my very eyes.

I fell backwards to the rooftop; you know the kind of fall that lasts a lifetime before you crash. I pushed out such a loud, hard scream as I fell that I imagined my throat would collapse before I was done yelling. Christ almighty—it was her—I mean she was it. Jasmine looked just like that thing I saw in the water. I pushed myself backward across the roof until I could go no further, the fear oozing out of me along with my breath.

"What kind of d-demon are you?"

My body told me to run, but what would I gain for it, only a trade of this monstrous beast for the filthy black water.

"No demon," the voice I heard was no longer Jasmine's. "Demons do not punish the wicked."

The beast took a step toward me, its talon-like toenails clattering on the shingles.

"You're no angel."

"I'm justice's arrow, fired at the guilty."

"You're the Reaper then?"

"No such thing, but you're getting closer."

Jasmine, or the beast that once was her, lunged in at me so fast I didn't have time to think or defend myself. I witnessed a blink of speed and felt the breeze of motion across my face. I turned at the waist—recoiled away. Suddenly, I felt an unexpected burning sensation in my stomach. I looked back at her as my hands patted down my belly. I saw her more clearly now, I should've been afraid—no terrified by what she was. Jasmine was a monster, and her hands were coated in my blood.

My stomach was torn wide open. Four slices ran horizontally across my belly and were so deep they each could fit one of my fingers to the knuckle. I should've dropped to my knees; how was I still standing? I watched the wolf-headed beast lumber back around me. It leaned into my face with its long snout. It was so close now I could gaze deep into its red eyes; it was like looking down a deep well, with nothing at the bottom but eternal darkness.

"Why, Jasmine?"

The beast cocked its head, as if to turn its ear to my words.

"All I wanted was to escape," I groaned in pain. "Escape."

She growled in my face, the scent of hell on her breath. I finally fell forward, face first into the peak of the roof. I felt myself begin to slide over. Anything but that, my mind felt one last shot of panic. I didn't want to die in that disgusting, mucky water. I refused to drown. I just couldn't know what my boys did when they died. My heart raced as I wearily tried to grasp something with my right hand. I felt my legs go off the edge of the roof. I would surely be in the water soon. Maybe I wouldn't drown. If I'm lucky these wounds kill me first. Suddenly, my motion stopped and then I snapped back up onto the roof like a rubber band.

"Not so fast," Jasmine slurred. "No escape for you, yet."

The sting of her bite was more excruciating than the cut of her claws. I felt each of her teeth, like metal train track spikes being driven into my thigh. Crunch. I heard my bones break, Jesus Christ, was she—

Oh no, oh God, she was eating me. A surge of pain exploded inside me. I felt every bite, each chew, every time my flesh tore and then nothing.

***

I awoke this morning in a cornfield, lying atop a puddle of thick, black mud. Just like I found Jasmine, I was stark naked. Up to my knees, I wiped my hand across the four jagged scars on my stomach: one for each of Jasmine's claws. I heard the roar of a tractor trailer's engine; I must've been close to the highway. I pushed through the tall growth until I found the metal legs of a tall billboard. I was only a few miles out of town, but still here. God, I was still here. I trashed my limbs about like a spoiled child as I shouted words I never used before. I cried for hours, finally punctuating my pain with one last scream, yet I found no relief in my twisting anguish.

The flood. I had nearly escaped; I was so close. Jasmine could've killed me, but she didn't, instead she cursed me to...to this. I was, as best I could tell, like her now. Blood under my fingernails, the taste of flesh on my tongue. If I was to ever know what I had become, demon or avenging angel, I would need to find her.

As I walked the old highway back into town, I sung out her name...Jasmine.

Jasmine...

<u>Accolades for Dark Water: Beaming Smile</u>

Dark Water: Beaming Smile was awarded Third Place in the Preditors and Editors Readers Polls 2011.

"Totally freaky, solid horror that's done with plot-driving intent, rather than with the intent to disgust the reader. Well done!" --Nola Sarina, author.

"This is a short novel, but it's extremely well written and riveting. If you like your horror with a bit of a spookier ambience and a serious level of anticipation, I recommend it. For me, it was the perfect levels of creepy vs. I just really NEEDed to know what exactly happened in those hours leading up to the flood." --Christi Snow, award-winning author.

"Kevin is both a storyteller and an artist, and that's evident in the art he creates: every picture tells a story that is both complex and subtle. I highly recommend him." --Jonathan Maberry, Bram Stoker award-winning author.

Website: www.kevinbreaux.com

Facebook: @author_kjb

Instagram: @author_kjb

Twitter: @author_kjb

www.ingramcontent.com/pod-product-compliance
Lightning Source LLC
Chambersburg PA
CBHW071502150726
48000CB00006B/2676